The Treasure of Ravenwood:
A Fairy Tale
by Barbara Lieberman

To my daughter, Ellie,
who asked for this fairy tale years
ago and who inspires me still

It stood in the midst of an ancient wood and the village had grown around it over the centuries. Even on bright days, it seemed shrouded in mist and mystery, silence and shadows. For all its great height and breadth, only the tallest tips of the towers stood above the ancient trees around it. The imposing iron fence that surrounded it had been built before living memory, no record of just who had forged it or built the castle.

There had always been a Master there. And, as is often the case when there are castles and masters and fences, there were stories and rumors. The truth had passed into the mist and all that remained was the feeling that the mist and the barrier guarded something... some sort of treasure.

Chapter One

"Hello." The girl was so startled by the voice, she dropped her basket, sending its contents all over the ground. As she gathered her things, one lone apple rolled through the fence. She watched it stop and looked up the length of a dark gray cloak to where a long hood covered someone's face.

"Did you speak to me just now?" she asked hesitantly.

"Yes," the deep voice answered. "I said hello to you. Did I frighten you?" The girl glanced at her basket.

"'Tis the truth, you did," she replied shyly. "But only because I never expected to find someone here. I've come here so many times and no one ever…"

I'm sorry I startled you," the cloaked figure interrupted quietly. "I have seen you here before and sought to meet you." The girl peered closely at it, trying to see a face or any sign of just who might be underneath all that grayness.

"Who are you?" she asked, still looking closely. The figure stood in the shadows just beyond the fence, which only added to the girl's difficulty in seeing him.

"I should ask you that first," the voice answered. "You are peering into *our* fence, after all." The girl shrugged.

"I'm called Mouse," she answered truthfully. "And, you?" The figure stood quietly for a moment before answering.

"*Called* Mouse," it repeated. "Is that not your name?" Mouse laughed a little.

"No, it's not. But, I have been called that for so long, I think of it that way." The long hood nodded slightly. "What is your name?"

"Since you have not shared your name, perhaps you should think of something to call me," the voice suggested. Mouse laughed again, feeling the conversation was slightly ridiculous.

"I shall have to think about that," she said cheerfully. "Do you know the Master of Ravenwood?" The hood nodded again.

"I do," it answered. Mouse decided it was a wonderful voice, deep and thrilling, and that it was mostly definitely male. "Do you know him, Mouse?" She laughed again.

"Of course not," she scoffed, feeling he was teasing her. "No one knows him. He lives behind this iron fence, after all, and never shows himself."

"True," the man answered. "And, why do you come to peer through his fence, Mouse? Do you seek to spy on my master? Or, just perhaps catch a glimpse of him?" Mouse shrugged and put her basket down.

"I have come to look through this fence for so long," she said wistfully. "I used to come and imagine what sort of man he was. But, now, I just come to look and think."

"And, what sort of man do you imagine?" Mouse smiled at her childish thoughts, wondering if this man could really care about them. Would he just tease her and think her a silly girl?

"I wonder why he needs such a fence," she shared, daring to open her thoughts with a stranger since no one else ever asked about them. "The people of the village all think there is some great treasure inside, you see. Something he is keeping all to himself. But, you probably know that."

"And, you, Mouse? What do you think?" Mouse's eyes narrowed as she pushed back the hood on her own cloak, looking around beyond the fence.

"I wonder at the need to keep people away," she answered, voicing thoughts long kept to her. "That's what a fence does, after all. It keeps people out… or in. It keeps him separate." The hood nodded again.

"Some fences are not made of iron," he said, sounding as if he were teasing again. "Your name, for example. It is a fence to protect you, I think." Mouse smirked and tilted her head.

"My name? How is that a fence?"

"It implies that you are small, meek and insignificant," he explained. "Perhaps you've decided it's better to let others think that, keeping the truth of yourself hidden behind that image. Perhaps you are not small and insignificant but quick, persistent, resourceful and canny, another way to look at a mouse." She smiled brightly, blushing a little, and rolled her eyes, unused to compliments from anyone but her father.

"Perhaps you are right," she said with a shrug. "I see what you mean. But, I *am* small." The man chuckled and nodded.

"You are, at that. Have you always lived in the village?" Mouse shook her head while still trying to get a better look at the cloaked man. It was difficult to examine him without staring rudely. On the other hand, he didn't make it any easier, being all covered and standing in the shadows.

"No, we came here when I was very young. My mother had just died and my father wanted to start over somewhere with fewer reminders of her. Then he married again. I started coming here shortly after that. To get away from… well, to be alone. Is that a problem? Will your master be very angry that I come? Will he be angry with you for speaking with me?"

"So many questions, little mouse," he said gently. "I do not believe my master will mind you coming just to look. I also do not think he will be angry with me. But, I shall ask him for you. You will, of course, have to return at least once more to hear his answer."

"I will," Mouse agreed."And perhaps I should ask him a question. Would you ask him how he is feeling? The figure was quiet for a moment.

"You wish to know how the master is feeling, Mouse? Why do you ask this?" Mouse looked around beyond the fence again, still only seeing the mist and shadows.

"Because I think he is alone," she said, not bothering to hide the sadness in her voice. "And, he may not have anyone to ask after him. It can be very lonely to have no one care enough to ask how one feels every once in a while." Mouse picked up her basket and smiled at the shrouded figure. "And, I shall call you 'Shadow'."

"Shadow?" he repeated, sounding surprised. "Why Shadow?"

"Because a shadow is here and yet not," she explained. "Another fence for a name. It is your name and yet it is not." He nodded slowly.

"I think I was right about your name, little mouse. Shadow I am, then. Until we meet again, be well." Because she could answer, shadow melted back into the bushes and disappeared.

"And, maybe you were not there at all…" Mouse said to herself. "Perhaps I imagined you after all." She pulled up her hood and dashed through the woods. She slipped through the kitchen door and tossed her cloak aside. Within moments, Mouse had the pastry rolled for meat pies for the evening meal.

"Where have you been all day, Mouse?" A large, overly-endowed woman swept into the kitchen and deposited herself on a chair, which groaned in protest. Mouse barely glanced up from her work.

"I had to go to the village for some fresh vegetables," she answered carefully, placing the pastry over meat pies and crimping the edges.

"That would not take all day." The older woman sniffed in annoyance, as she fluffed her silky skirt and picked away imaginary bits. From the day she married John the Tailor, Constance ran his household, with Mouse as her personal servant, cook, maid and scapegoat. John, of course, did not know this, as Constance let him believe she cooked and cleaned and mended for the family. And, as long as Mouse cooperated, Constance didn't beat her. Unfortunately for Mouse, the meaning of 'cooperate' could change with no notice.

John had married again, to offer his little daughter a sense of normalcy after her mother's death. He'd thought to give her a mother and sisters, a home, and a sense of belonging that had been lost for him when his own parents had died. He also knew a loving wife made for a happy home, though he'd missed the mark on that with Constance.

"I'm sorry, Mother," Mouse choked out. She would never think of the bloated, nasty woman as her mother. Her stepmother insisted on the endearment, however, and Mouse tried to use it occasionally to avoid yet another beating. "I didn't realize you were looking for me. I have been back for some time."

"And, you did not hear me calling you?" Constance asked, picking at some fruit in Mouse's basket. "Or you chose to ignore me?"

"I must have been distracted," Mouse offered quickly. She placed the apple tart in the oven and wiped her damp forehead on her apron.

"You are always distracted, Mouse," Constance snapped. "I have not beaten you for some time. I see I have been remiss." She stood with difficulty and left the kitchen. Mouse sighed and sat down, leaning her elbows on the table. The kitchen was the warmest room in the house, due to the ovens, and Mouse closed her eyes and enjoyed being warm. She never minded being cold when out walking to the village or exploring the woods by herself. At night, in bed, was another thing entirely and then she minded the cold a great deal. It seeped into her skin and then her bones, making her shiver and her teeth chatter. Sometimes she feared the cold would seep into her heart and that she might never feel warm again. But, now, she had warm thoughts of a new friend to keep her company. ..

Chapter Two

Mouse placed the meat pies on the table, along with a pitcher of fresh milk and another of ale. Having marked one pie in particular, Mouse placed that at her father's place. She was always careful to give him the best of whatever she made, In this case the pie with the most meat. It was her way of taking care of him, even if he never knew it was her.

A kind and gentle man, John the Tailor loved his daughter and never failed to let her know. This had been more difficult since he married Constance but he still made the effort. Constance had two daughters of her own when she married Mouse's father and they always took priority, at least in Constance's mind. They were older and prettier and had everything they wanted. Mouse wore their castoffs and saw to their needs. She was often reminded of the fairy tale of the girl with the wicked stepmother and stepsisters as she tended to their demands. It was an image that brought a smile to Mouse's face, for there was always the hope a fairy godmother would change *her* life as well. And unlike the girl who slept in the ashes, Mouse still had her beloved father.

"The food at last," Constance said impatiently. "John, do come to the table. I have made you meat pies this evening, though your daughter dawdles and allows them to get cold." Mouse's father came into the room and smiled at his daughter as she poured his ale.

"And, how is my mouse?" he asked, as he sat at his place at the head of the table.

"Fine, Papa," she assured him with a smile. "And, you, how was your day?" He winked at her, warming her heart.

"It was a good day," he said with a nod. "But any day you wake up is a good day, Mouse." Constance's two daughters arrived a moment later, making a grand entrance as always, and sat across from Mouse. Tall and brown-haired like their mother, the girls apparently got their good looks from their father. Slim and fair, eyes like whiskey, perfect skin that was never touched by sunlight if they could avoid it… They were both beautiful, by any standards, though the eldest was by far the loveliest of the two… to look at.

Not for the first time, Mouse wondered if two people could be any more inappropriately named than her stepsisters. Purity and Charity sat quietly while John said grace and then pounced, yes, pounced on their pies. Mouse rolled her eyes and picked at her own. Constance had no idea that John's pie had the lion's share of meat and that thought alone helped Mouse enjoy her meal, the eating habits of her sister's notwithstanding.

"We should send the message soon, husband," Constance stated, dabbing daintily at her lips. "Purity should be married with all due haste, given her age, and she only wishes him for a husband."

"Constance, we know nothing of him, "John said wearily. "How can she desire a man she has never met or even seen? What makes you think, even if he would agree, that he is a suitable husband?" The older woman let out an exasperated sigh.

"We have been over this and over this, John. Be a man, for once. You have agreed that the girls are to be married in order of their ages. Purity wants the Master of Ravenwood for a husband and have him she shall. What better bride than she to benefit from whatever treasure the man is hoarding?"

"Suppose he is old and decrepit?" John asked mockingly. Mouse almost choked on her mouthful.

"Then she shall inherit it all that much sooner," Constance answered, having clearly already thought the same thing. "Send the message. Make her the finest dress in the village for her audience with him. Her beauty alone will win him over." Mouse kept her eyes on her meal to avoid looking at anyone else.

All girls of marriageable age, at one time or another, dreamed of marrying the Master of Ravenwood. The village was named after the estate, after all, and everyone believed he was rich beyond imagining. Did he not purchase food, ale, cloth and more from the villagers, always paid for in gold, never in need of credit? It was also believed he was alone and therefore in need of a wife. Message after message had been sent to the castle over the years, only to be ignored by the Master. Mouse assumed this message would be ignored as well. But, Constance and her daughters would have to learn this, as had all the other disappointed girls who had gone on to marry men in the village.

"Keven, the cooper's son, has spoken to me again," John said, glancing at Mouse. "He still presses his suit for Mouse." Constance glared at the girl.

"You agreed, husband. They are to be married in the order of their ages. Purity is eighteen and she should be married first. Charity is seventeen and Mouse only sixteen. She can wait." Mouse looked up at her father, her eyes wide and pleading.

"Oh, yes, Papa, you agreed. You did." She had no desire to marry anyone, let alone Keven Cooper. He nodded slowly as he ate.

"I did," he agreed, looking over his daughter's stricken face. Her blond braid was tightly bound around her head and covered with a wrinkled house cap. Her small frame was hidden beneath an old dress two sizes too big but even that did not hide her appeal. A sweet face with bright blue eyes, a small freckled nose, a sweet mouth that was usually smiling; his daughter's face was all of her mother, as was her deceptively small size. He had only to look at Mouse to see his first wife again. He knew his daughter did not want the cooper's son, as surely as he knew the boy wanted his daughter. "I'll send the message to Ravenwood," he said finally, "But we should not get our hopes up too high."

"And, you'll make me a dress, Father?" Purity asked eagerly. "A beautiful dress that will be better than all the others have?" He nodded again as he finished his dinner. "Blue, to show off my hair and eyes? Soft and flowing and rich looking? I must look the part..." Mouse jumped up to fetch the apple tart from the kitchen. She sliced it and passed her father the first piece.

"A fine dress you shall have," he assured Purity. "If he agrees to meet with you." After his slice was gone, Mouse brought him his pipe. John squeezed her hand in thanks before she began clearing the table.

"Why do you not wear the dresses I made for you, Mouse? "

"They are much too fine to wear when I... *help* Constance," Mouse answered, trying to be as truthful as possible. "I am saving them for special occasions." John frowned at her as she left the room, feeling as if he were missing something important, but he let her go, retreating to his own room to read a bit before sleep. Mouse retreated into the warm kitchen. She didn't mind the work there, as it kept her from her cold, lonely room.

Chapter Three

Slipping through the trees, Mouse stopped several times and watched carefully to be sure no one had followed her. Finally, she stepped from the woods near the corner of the fence that surrounded Ravenwood. It had been several days since she first met Shadow and Mouse was anxious to speak with him again.

She'd gone to the village first so that her basket was full with fresh things for the household meals. Except for the fear that she'd run into Keven, Mouse always enjoyed her trips to the village shops. She didn't mind if there were lines at the stands for fresh fruit and vegetables, or at the butcher shop for fresh meats, because she could relax and enjoy her time away from Constance and her stepsisters. Everyone greeted her by name, always asked after her father and, reluctantly, after Constance, and wished her a good day, thanking her in return for her own good wishes for them. She usually took her time, extending her tasks as long as she dared. Today, though, she'd moved more quickly, chatted a little less, and moved through the purchases with as much haste as she'd dared, so she could head up the hill.

"Hello, little mouse." Mouse pushed back her hood and smiled as the cloaked figure stepped from the shadows beyond the fence. She still could see nothing but the voluminous cloak.

"Hello, Shadow. How are you this beautiful day?" He stepped closer to the fence.

"Most people would say it is damp and dreary today, Mouse." She smiled and rolled her eyes.

"Papa says it's a good day if you wake up. And, it is a beautiful day because you have come to meet me. Tell me, did you ask your master my question?" Shadow nodded slowly.

"I did. And, he was most pleased you asked. In fact, that was his answer. He said to tell you he is feeling very pleased you thought to ask." Mouse clasped her hands in front of her and sighed, rather delighted with that answer.

"See, Shadow? He did need someone to ask. That is truly remarkable, that I could please the Master of Ravenwood, isn't it? And, you doubted it was a beautiful day."

"I did not doubt it for a moment, Mouse," he corrected her. "I simply pointed out that others might not agree with you and me on the matter." Mouse laughed and put down her basket.

"And, you, are you well, Shadow?" Mouse wrapped her hands around the fence uprights. He nodded.

"I am, now that you are here again." Mouse felt a small, unfamiliar thrill pass through her at his words. "Are you well?"

"I am," she assured him. "Now that I see you again. I thought I might have imagined you. But, was your master angry with you at all? Did he say I could visit you again and look through his fence?" Shadow chuckled softly.

"He was not angry at all," he assured her. "And, you may look to your heart's content, Mouse."

"That is a great deal of looking," she warned him with a grin. "And will you visit with me when I come to look? Somehow, it won't be the same to just look, if you aren't here to share it with me."

"I may visit with you," he told her. "The master has said I may if I wish to and I do." Mouse gave that answer some thought.

"It is a truly remarkable day then, "she said, smiling brightly. "I have a new friend. I do, don't I, Shadow? You are to be my friend?" He nodded again.

"I am that," he agreed. "And are you mine, little mouse?" She nodded enthusiastically.

"Oh, yes," she said, suddenly turning more serious. "And, as your friend, I feel I must warn you. Constance is insisting that Papa send a message to your master. She seeks to introduce her daughter to him in hopes of marriage, you see." Shadow folded his hands in front of him. Actually, Mouse assumed that is what he did. The sleeves of the cloak were so long, they covered his hands.

"I see," Shadow said quietly. "And, who is Constance, that she would ask your father to do this?" Mouse laughed self-consciously.

"I'm sorry," she apologized. "Let me explain. My father married Constance so she is my stepmother. She insists I call her 'Mother' but I just cannot think of her that way. She has two daughters and it is the eldest she seeks to wed to your master."

"Ah, I see now. And what do you think of this idea?" Mouse smirked and rolled her blue eyes heavenward.

"I think nothing will come of it," she said truthfully. "Every girl in Ravenwood has entertained these notions, only to marry a boy from the village when your master ignores the messages. I don't think it will be any different this time."

"And, do you *harbor such notions*, Mouse? Do you wish to marry the Master of Ravenwood?" Mouse shrugged.

"I don't wish to marry anyone. I have never met him. I don't understand why everyone assumes he wants to marry or needs to. Perhaps he is already married and that is why he ignores the messages. Perhaps he is old and decrepit. I have not thought of such things for myself."

"Have you not? Then you were not completely correct when you said *every* girl in Ravenwood harbors such thoughts. Is there a boy in the village whom you fancy, Mouse?" She laughed at that.

"No," came the emphatic reply. "The cooper's son has pressed his suit to my father but Constance insists we be married in order of our ages. 'Tis the only thing I like about her, as it means I will be forced to marry last. And given her daughters…" Mouse stopped and blushed brightly.

"What is it you were saying?" Shadow prompted, when she did not continue. Mouse bit her lip.

"It would not do to speak my mind concerning those two, particularly if your master considers meeting… well, he should make up his own mind, shouldn't he? Not be swayed by my opinions?" Shadow chuckled again.

"You are an unusual young woman, Mouse," he said quite sincerely. "I find myself very interested in your opinion of your stepsisters but I shall wait until you are ready to share it with me." Mouse bent down and reached into her basket, withdrawing an apple.

"I brought you this," she said, holding it out t the fence. "I thought to bring you something and had little to offer. Would you like it? 'Tis the best of the bushel." Shadow reached out but only his sleeve brushed Mouse's hand as he took the apple.

"You thought to bring me something?" he asked, his voice surprised. "I thank you, Mouse. You are most kind."

"You are most welcome," she said brightly. "And, could you ask your master another question for me? I should ask after him again, don't you think?"

"I think that would be very nice of you," Shadow agreed. "What shall I ask this time?" Mouse mulled that over for a moment.

"I really should have thought again, shouldn't I?" she said, laughing at herself. "Perhaps you could ask him if there is anything he needs. Yes, that's it. Ask him if there is anything he needs." Shadow chuckled again. Mouse found she liked very much that she could make him laugh.

"If that is what you wish me to ask, I shall do so," he replied with a nod of his hood. Mouse picked up her basket and looked around through the fence one last time.

"I must get back before Constance misses me," she said sadly. "If she finds me gone, she'll… well, I shall come back as soon as I can, Shadow." He nodded again.

"I shall look for you. Be well, little mouse."

Chapter Four

Mouse cleared the table and washed the dishes, again enjoying the warmth of the kitchen. The weather was changing and soon there would be little warmth to be found anywhere in the house, except in the bedrooms on the second floor. Since Mouse slept in the attic, she would be quite cold over the winter months. Normally, she did not mind sleeping there, as she could be alone with her thoughts and dreams, away from Constance's dogged attention. But, she did mind the attic in winter.

Climbing the stairs to the attic, Mouse went to the window and leaned on the casement. Though small, the single window allowed her a view of the village below as well as the forest beyond it. And, beyond that, lay Ravenwood and Shadow.

Mouse wondered if he had spoken to his master and delivered her message. It was so thrilling to have a friend all her own, even if he were a little bit mysterious. Someone no one else knew and someone who seemed to enjoy her company. Shadow was certainly a refreshing change from the cooper's son.

Keven had pursued Mouse for several years, to her dismay. He was nice enough looking, even bothering to bathe now and then, an unusual trait compared to most boys in the village. He was eighteen years old and had learned his father's craft, assuring his future as a provider for this family. He had his teeth, another plus, she thought with a wry smile. These were all the qualities girls and families ticked off the invisible list when considering a future husband. Mouse's list was of a different nature entirely. Keven lacked imagination. He never spoke of hopes or dreams. He wanted a wife to fix his meals, share his bed, and give him children... and little else.

Mouse sighed and changed into her old sleeping gown. It trailed on the floor, as she moved to her small bed and wrapped her thin blanket around her. She had left her stockings on to keep her feet warmer and, as she drifted off to sleep, Mouse hoped it would not snow just yet. She wanted to visit Ravenwood a few more times before winter came to stay.

Chapter Five

Slipping from the forest, Mouse peered through the iron uprights and hoped Shadow was waiting for her. She wondered how he knew she was there on her previous visits or if he waited for her every day. That last thought disturbed her.

"Something wrong, Mouse?" he asked, as he appeared before her. She smiled and shrugged.

"I was just wondering about you," she told him. "I was wondering if you knew somehow that I was here or if you waited for me every day. I did not like the thought of you waiting here by yourself on the days I cannot be here."

"Do not worry yourself on my account," Shadow said, folding his hands in front of him. "I have much to occupy my time, though nothing as pleasant as your visits."

"And, did you ask the master my question," she asked hopefully, feeling that now-familiar thrill that Shadow enjoyed her company as much as she did his.

"I did," he assured her with a nod, "and he said to tell you that he has all he needs and to thank you for your kindness." Mouse sighed contentedly.

"Remarkable," she said, smiling brightly. "Isn't it remarkable that he should thank me, Shadow?"

"Not really, Mouse. It was kind of you to ask. Most would ask one such as my master what he could do for them and not concern themselves with his needs. It is you who are remarkable, I think." Mouse blushed and shook her head.

"No, not I," she said quietly. "There is nothing remarkable about me. But, you, Shadow, do you need anything?" He chuckled softly and shook his head.

"All I need, my master provides," he told her. "And, I have everything I need, now that I have you for a friend, little mouse." She blushed again and looked at the ground.

"Do you truly feel that way about me?" she asked quietly, and then she put up her hand. "No, don't answer that. I should not have asked you to repeat it. That was greedy of me. It is just that no one has ever said such things to me and it does feel nice, doesn't it? When someone likes you?" Shadow nodded.

"It does," he agreed. "I wonder, if you would tell me of your stepsisters today? I have been wondering what you would say of them since we last spoke together." Mouse shrugged and considered his request a moment.

"I tend to… speak my mind, Shadow," she began hesitantly. "And, if I were to speak of them, I fear you would no longer like me. I cannot be quite… *kind*… about them, you see, and you may think me mean-spirited as a result. I have only just won your friendship and I would hate to lose it over my opinion of them." Shadow chuckled and shook his head.

"You amuse me, little mouse. And you could not possibly lose my friendship by telling me about them. I promise to listen for the truth in your words." Mouse sighed and looked up at the gray sky.

"Their names are Purity and Charity," she began, still fearing her words would end her friendship. "And two more inappropriately named people you will never meet. Purity is eighteen and beautiful. 'Tis the truth, she is the most beautiful girl in the village. But, you see, she knows it and that is the problem. She spends the entire day looking in the mirror to see if she is still beautiful or perhaps even more beautiful. Now, I suppose I am being uncharitable because, if I were beautiful, I would probably worry about it going away and spend the entire day checking that it had not. But, I'm not beautiful, so I cannot possibly understand spending so much time looking at one's own face. Can you, Shadow?"

"No, I cannot," he agreed solemnly. Mouse sighed again.

"And, so, everything Purity does and thinks has to do with her beauty," Mouse continued. "She asks Papa to make her dresses in colors to compliment her hair and her eyes. She pinches her cheeks to make them pinker and bites her lips to make them redder. She darkens her brows and lashes with kohl and even checks her reflection in windows and bath water. She never thinks of anyone else, just her own face. It seems a waste of life, don't you think?"

"I do," Shadow agreed. "And, Charity, what is she like?" Mouse frowned intently.

"Seventeen and also very beautiful. Shadow, have you ever met a man, a truly handsome man, and when he began to speak, he became ugly?" Shadow nodded.

"I have, Mouse. And, is this how your stepsister is?" Mouse nodded.

"Truly beautiful until she opens her mouth. Not a single kind, thoughtful word passes those pink lips. Charity criticizes everything and everyone. Nothing suits, nothing pleases, and nothing is good enough for Charity. Papa makes her dresses exactly as she requests but she finds fault with each of them. The food is never hot enough or spiced properly. The boys are never handsome enough or rich enough. The day is either too hot or too cold, too fair or too dark. I do believe that if she were to face the Lord himself, He would not suit Charity. It must be very unhappy for her, don't you think, Shadow, to never find anything or anyone she likes?"

"It must be," Shadow agreed. "Unhappy for those trying to please her as well, is it not, Mouse?"

"'Tis the truth," she agreed with another sigh. "And, now, you will think I am a most terribly unkind person for what I have said to you. You won't tell your master, will you? If he should agree to meet Purity, he should keep his own counsel regarding her suitability as a wife, shouldn't he?" Shadow was quiet for a moment.

"I serve my master, Mouse," he said thoughtfully. "Would you have me keep this truth from him, knowing it as I do?" She chewed her lip thoughtfully.

"No, that would not be right," she agreed. "But 'tis only my opinion of them. If you are to share it with him, will you tell him that? So, then he will only consider it as such and not as fact?" Shadow nodded.

"I will indeed," he assured her. "For all you speak of them plainly and honestly," he continued, "you still notice their unhappiness. Few would see past the unpleasantness to what lies beneath, Mouse. You still speak with kindness toward them, and with love, despite their flaws." Mouse was not sure what to make of that compliment. "Tell me, then, if your father is a tailor, why your sisters wear new dresses made to suit their whims and you wear their castoffs?" Mouse blushed and looked down at her dress.

"How did you know this was a castoff?" she asked, suddenly embarrassed as she pulled her cloak more tightly around her.

"It is much too large," Shadow observed, to her further dismay, "and, clearly made for someone else. Forgive me for speaking of it, I did not mean to embarrass you, which I have so obviously done. I only wondered why your father does not make such garments for you."

"He makes dresses for me," she said, barely above a whisper, still not looking at Shadow. "But, they are too fine to wear when I cook and clean. And the village roads are too dusty or muddy for their fine hems. I keep them tucked away for special occasions."

"Do special occasions ever arise, Mouse?" The hood tilted to one side. "Or do you work so hard keeping house for your stepmother that you never get to wear a pretty dress?" Mouse looked up, frowning intently.

"How did you know that?" she asked worriedly, narrowing her eyes at him. "If she were to learn anyone knew I did all the work, she would…" Mouse bit her tongue and looked at the ground again. "You are right, of course, but 'tis not so very awful. The kitchen is warm, even in winter, and I can see that Papa gets the best cuts of meat and the most broth, if I make and serve the meals." She sighed again and looked up at Shadow. I must go back," she said sadly. "And, when the snows come, I won't be able to come again for some time."

"I understand," Shadow assured her. "You will come until then?" Mouse smiled a little, pleased he still wanted her to visit him.

"I will try," she said, looking him over. "Won't you tell me your name now?" Shadow tilted his head again, or at least, the hood tilted.

"Will you tell me yours?" Mouse had the distinct feeling he was teasing her. She laughed and shook her head.

"I don't think I will just yet," she said impishly. "And, I prefer to think of you as my Shadow. It keeps you mine alone since it is a name only we share." Shadow laughed, to her delight, and nodded.

"And, though everyone else calls you Mouse, I think if you that way as well. Be well, my little mouse. And, hurry home so Constance does not beat you for being late." Mouse opened her mouth to speak but Shadow disappeared before she could reply.

Chapter Six

It was several weeks before Mouse was able to sneak away to the Ravenwood estate. She hurried through the forest and approached the fence, trying not to slip on the snow. Only a small amount had fallen the night before but there was just enough on the ground to make it treacherous going in places. The infernal mud did not help the situation.

"Hello, my Mouse." She smiled brightly in response.

"Hello, my Shadow. Are you well?"

"I am," he assured her. "As is my master. He bids me wish you well and ask how you are." Mouse grinned from ear to ear.

"Remarkable," she said with a happy sigh, "that he should think of me before I even arrive. Please tell him I am also well. I am sorry I have been away for so long. I have been unable to get away from Constance. She seems to sense I am up to something and is keeping a close watch on me. I am, after up, up to something, so it is difficult for me to hide my desire to get away." Mouse rolled her eyes at her own foolishness.

"I understand," he assured her, "though I have missed you, Mouse. The days do not seem as beautiful without you." Mouse blushed as she set her basket on the ground and wrapped her hands around the frigid iron uprights of the fence.

"Has your master received my father's message?" she asked, wondering if she should. Shadow nodded.

"He has," he told her. "Along with several more from other fathers. He is considering them all." Mouse did not even bother to attempt to hide her surprise.

"I always thought he just tossed them aside and gave them no thought," she said truthfully. "I never once considered that he would actually pay them any mind." Shadow chuckled.

"He considers every message he receives," he explained. "To do otherwise would be most thoughtless, would it not?" Mouse nodded.

"It would," she agreed, "and I should not have thought that of him. I truly did not mean it that way. I just felt he might find such requests unwanted and unwelcome, as I find them when directed at me." Shadow suddenly stepped closer.

"Does someone make unwelcome requests of you, Mouse?" She could hear the concern in his voice and it touched her deeply.

"The cooper's son still seeks my attention," she admitted with a bright blush. "'Tis the other reason I have been unable to visit you sooner. Any chance to find me alone and he seeks to gain my affection. I must tell you, 'tis most unsettling." Still blushing, Mouse gazed up at the gray sky. "Why must I wed, anyway? It all seems such a waste."

"Marriage… a waste?" Shadow asked. "Do you not seek love as others do?" Mouse shrugged.

"One does not seek love," she told him, "it should find you all on its own. And, though affection may grow from a marriage that is arranged, I doubt true love does."

"Such wisdom from one so young," Shadow mused. "This boy does not hold your affection, then?" Mouse snorted in a most unladylike fashion at that thought.

"Hardly," she muttered. "But he knows Constance will not allow me to marry until the others do. So, he seeks to… bind a promise to one another."

"In what way does he do this?" Shadow asked. Mouse wondered why his voice suddenly sounded so strange.

"He tries to… to kiss me and to…" She blushed and glanced at the cloaked figure. "You are a man, are you not?" Shadow actually laughed.

"Yes, Mouse, I am." She nodded, her imaginings confirmed.

"You do know what men do, when they want a woman?" She was blushing so furiously now, she felt her cheeks might truly burst into flame.

"I see," he said quietly. "Tell me, Mouse, do you feel unsafe with him?" She considered that.

"I do," she admitted. "That is why I had to be so careful about coming back. I'm afraid that he will seek to… to force my affection." Shadow made a sound that Mouse could only describe as a grunt, a sound of disgust that perfectly reflected her own feelings on the subject of Keven Cooper's attentions.

"Have you told your father your fears?" he asked after a moment. Mouse shook her head.

"I rarely see him alone," she admitted. "And Constance would only see this as assurance I will marry when the time comes. She will want me out of the house as soon as the others are married off."

"Perhaps you are wrong about that," Shadow suggested. "If you were to be married off, who would do the work for Constance that you do now? Remind her that, should you become someone else's wife, she will have no one to do her chores for her. This may protect you from the cooper's son. Tell her of his unwanted advances and remind her of the unfortunate consequences to you, and to her, if he is successful." Mouse smiled and nodded thoughtfully.

"A good idea, that," she agreed. "You are quite clever, Shadow. Have I told you how happy I am that you are my friend?"

"Your friendship also pleases me, Mouse. And, if I have helped you in even the slightest measure, I am pleased with that as well."

"I should go," Mouse said, reaching for her basket. "I brought you something else today. 'Tis just a tart I made last night. Perhaps you could share a taste with your master as well. Only a taste, though, as I mean this for you." She reached through the fence to give him the tart and, when he took it from her, he kept her hand. His fingers were warm against her chilled ones and Mouse's eyes widened as he lifted her hand and kissed it. When he released her, Mouse withdrew it and held her hand against her cheek, still feeling his warmth on her cold skin.

"Be well, my mouse," he whispered, "and be safe." Shadow slipped back into the darkness and Mouse stood rooted to the spot, her hand still to her cheek and her heart warmed beyond measure.

Chapter Seven

"Where have you been, Mouse?" Keven Cooper stepped from the trees as Mouse turned from the fence. Her face drained of color as she wondered just how long he had been standing there.

"Just walking," she said, her voice strained with the lie. "Did you follow me?" Keven laughed as he stepped closer.

"Your stepmother is looking for you," he warned her, a little too cheerfully. "I offered to come and find you. I've seen you slipping away to the forest before. T'was easy to follow your tracks in the snow and mud. Tell me, Mouse, what are you doing here in the corner of Ravenwood. Dreaming of the master? Wondering if he'll choose you for a wife?" Mouse took a slow, deep breath, as much to think as to buy time.

"Absolutely not," she said, quite honestly. "And, you know full well I am not to be wed yet. Now, if you will excuse me, I will be going home. I do not relish a beating today." Keven blocked her way and Mouse glared up at him. Though not particularly tall for a boy his age, he was still much taller than the very short Mouse.

"But, I have only just found you," he said, looking her over slowly and showing no signs of moving out of her way. "And you are so cold. Perhaps I could warm you up a bit." Mouse's face certainly flamed at that suggestion. She took a step back toward the fence and shook her head.

"I am quite comfortable in this cloak, pulling it more tightly around her for good measure. "And, the walk back will warm me quite enough. I am in no need of your assistance." Keven stepped closer, the devil in his eyes, and smiled. Mouse couldn't help but wonder why he was even pursuing her. His looks and future would gain him any girl in the village.

"'Tis a game you play with me," he said, a warning in his voice, "and I tire of it. You want me just as much of the others do and I always get what I want. Just a kiss, now, to show you the way of it…" Mouse scoffed loudly and held her basket between them, meager shield that it was.

"I would think you desire a more willing participant for your demonstration," she said, not bothering to hide her disgust or impatience. "I do not wish to kiss you and that is the truth of it. 'Tis no game." He stepped closer, his hand now on the fence over her head. Mouse saw too late she'd backed herself into a trap. "Please don't do this. Seek a girl who wishes your affections. You'd be much happier with someone else. I am not the girl for you…" Keven grabbed her suddenly, causing Mouse to cry out and drop her basket. He pulled her against him, even as she was trapped against the fence and she knew a panic she'd never felt before. Just as quickly, Mouse felt him release her, causing her to stumble. When she looked at Keven, he was pinned with his back against the fence.

"Go home, Mouse," Shadow whispered. She took off through the woods without a backward glance.

Chapter Eight

Mouse raced into the kitchen and tossed her cloak aside. She gathered everything to begin the evening meal, in the hopes it would look as if she had been there for some time. Only too late did she realize she had left her basket behind at Ravenwood. Salvaging what she could, Mouse made a stew and set it to heat over the fire. She punched down the dough she made earlier that morning and set it in several pans, putting those in the oven. Only when the meal preparations were completed did Mouse sit and begin to breathe again. Then, she began to shake.

How had Shadow known she was in trouble? Perhaps he waited to see that she was safely away before returning to his master. Whatever his reasons, he had saved her from Keven's clutches. How would she ever repay his assistance?

"Where have you been, girl?" Constance demanded. She clouted Mouse in the head and glared at the girl. "Sitting here as if you had servants of your own? A lady of leisure, are you?" Mouse shook her head, as much to clear it as to deny the charge.

"I only just sat down," she said honestly. Her head was still ringing from the hard blow and she closed her eyes a moment to still the spinning. "The meal is prepared and warming. The bread is baking. I will set the table now." As she stood, Constance smacked her across the face.

"You will not talk back to me, you little strumpet! I know you run off to dally with the cooper's son and he will have you for good once my girls are properly wed." Mouse leaned against the table, for fear the spinning kitchen would overtake her.

"But who will care for you and Papa then?" she asked meekly, hoping she sounded earnest. "I had thought to stay behind and keep your house for you both." Constance's eyes narrowed at the small person in front of her.

"Did you?" she asked, clearly not having thought of this before. "Well, don't dally with the boys, then, else you'll end up bed and wed before you cut the biscuits."

"I swear I do not dally with the boys in the village," Mouse assured her. "Could you not help me keep Keven at bay, so I could stay here? Perhaps tell him I may never marry and that he should seek a different wife? He would be a fine match for Charity, perhaps. If the Master of Ravenwood chooses Purity, you could suggest Keven for Charity." Constance looked Mouse's pale, hopeful face over suspiciously.

"You're up to something, Mouse," an accusation clear in her voice. "Keven Cooper has no interest in you as of this very afternoon. So, either you have convinced him of your lack of interest or he has had you already and sees no reason to linger over you. Either way, you seem to be free of him." Mouse's eyes widened.

"How do you know this?" she gasped, and gripped the table as the dizziness continued.

"He seems to think you *bewitched*," Constance said with a haughty sniff, looking over Mouse with distaste. "Seems something happened to him for which he blames you. I always did think you touched by the fey ones. This will stop *any* man from wanting you, for sure. You may just get your wish and stay here with me forever." At that, Constance clouted Mouse again and left the room laughing. Mouse sat down again and wondered just what had happened when she ran away from Ravenwood.

Chapter Nine

When Mouse climbed the stairs to her room later that night, her head was still spinning. Constance had been unhappy with the stew and knocked Mouse in the head several more times when she was washing up after the meal. Because the snow had begun to fall shortly after dark, the small attic was colder than ever and Mouse shivered as she undid her braid and brushed her hair. The meager blanket would do little to warm her tonight and Mouse thought to return to the kitchen for her cloak before changing for bed…

"Mouse?" Whirling at the sound of a familiar voice, in her attic room of all places, Mouse missed the candle wick she was attempting to light. She whirled around at the sound and a wave of dizziness passed over her. Surely she'd imagined that voice in her room, closing her eyes against the pain and nausea. Constance must have hit her much harder than she'd realized.

"Mouse?" She opened her eyes and gasped as she saw Shadow in the corner of her room.

"Shadow? What are you doing here? Did anyone see you? However did you get up into my attic?"His hood moved slowly from one side to the other at her many questions.

"What's wrong, my mouse? Did the boy find you and hurt you after all?" Mouse sank to her bed and closed her eyes, then opened them again to see if he were really there.

"No," she answered weakly, still not really sure he was there. She lit the candle, finally, and lo and behold, there stood Shadow. "He returned home and has apparently changed his mind about me. What did you do to him?" Shadow chuckled and shrugged.

"I did nothing but pin him to the fence," he admitted. "When he turned to look at me, I melted back into the shadows. He never saw me and drew his own conclusions." Mouse allowed herself a small smile.

"And, so, he thinks I bewitched him," she said, putting a hand to her aching head. "He has told everyone he wants nothing to do with me as a result. I owe you a great deal for that, as well as our good advice. Constance no longer seeks to marry me off in any great hurry." Shadow nodded.

"That is good, at least," he agreed quietly. "Though you may come to regret that, if you change your mind about marrying in the future. But, why are you so unwell, little mouse?" She looked over at him.

"Constance was unhappy with me today," she explained weakly, pulling the blanket around her. "And, when she is unhappy with me…"

"Ah, I see," Shadow said, nodding. "I brought back your basket." He pulled it from his cloak and set it on the floor. "Why have you no fire, Mouse, and only one small thin blanket?" She shrugged.

"I'm fine," she lied, not really wanting to talk about that. "But, why have you come here? You should not have risked it. You should go before anyone sees you." Mouse stood suddenly, wondering again how he had gotten into her room, let alone into her house unseen.

"I must be sure you are well first," he said, taking a step toward her. "And my master wishes to know if there is anything you need." Mouse's eyes grew wide at that.

"Truly?" she asked in awe. "Remarkable. But, no, there is nothing I need. Except for you to go, Shadow. You must go back before anyone sees you. I couldn't bear if anything happened to you."

"Mouse, my master could give you anything you need. Wood for a fire, thick warm blankets, gold, anything. You have but to tell me and he will give you whatever it is you ask him for." Mouse shook her head, in spite of her headache.

"No," she insisted. "I have all I need. Your master has given me a gift beyond gold and I will ask no more of him. But, you must go. Please! I beg you, please go! The people in the village are in awe of Ravenwood but they are also afraid of what they do not know. If they should find you, they might take advantage of you and your master in some awful way. The treasure is always uppermost in their minds. Please go and go safely."

"I will go, Mouse," he assured her. "But tell me first, what has my master given you that is so valuable? I know of no such gift." Mouse smiled at him and tilted her head.

"Don't you?" she asked, her eyes lighting up just a little. "'Tis you he has given me. And, I can only be happy if I know you are safe behind the fence. You are my priceless gift and I must not let anything happen to you, Shadow, for I love you as no other."

"I?" he asked, his voice suddenly strained.

"Yes, yes," Mouse said impatiently. "But please go now! I will come again when the snows are gone but go before they hear you!" Shadow took another step toward her.

"Blow out the candle, Mouse." She frowned but did as he instructed. "Now, Mouse, close your eyes." Still frowning, she closed her eyes and wondered what he was up to. She felt the warmth of his wool cloak against her as Shadow drew her up into his arms. His warm fingers tilted her chin up and she felt his mouth close over hers. Warm, soft, and thoroughly disconcerting, Shadow kissed her. The pain in her head forgotten, Mouse felt his warm flow into her and welcomed his kiss. Lifting her from the floor, he placed her on her small bed and kissed her again.

"Good night, my mouse," he whispered. He kissed her forehead, her nose, and then her lips. Then, he disappeared into the darkness. Mouse sat up and lit her candle, still feeling very warm. She found Shadow's cloak draped across her, covering her to her toes and beyond.

***

By the time the light began to filter through Mouse's window the next morning, the snows had drifted deeply against the buildings in the village. Mouse woke slowly, still feeling warm and cozy wrapped in Shadow's cloak. The enormous garment was made of the finest, softest wool she had ever touched. Reluctantly slipping her feet from beneath the cloak, Mouse sat on the side of her bed and held the soft material to her cheek. The cloak and her basket were the only things keeping Mouse from believing it had all been a dream.

But, if it hadn't been a dream, then Shadow had really come to her. He had held her and kissed her. The memory of his kiss and the feelings it evoked caused Mouse to blush, as she folded the cloak on her bed. Tucking it under her mattress, she dressed quickly in the frigid room and dashed down the stairs to make the morning meal. The snows would last for several months now and she had only the cloak and memory of that kiss to keep her warm.

Chapter Ten

As Mouse put the morning porridge on the table, her father smiled at her. She smiled back before returned to the kitchen for the bread and jam.

"I do believe the thaw's begun," John said, when Mouse returned to the dining room. "And Spring will arrive earlier this year."

"The thaw brings mud," Charity complained. "And, that will ruin my new cloak. I hate the thaw."

"You hate the snow as well," Purity reminded her. "And, the spring. Why is it you hate the spring?"

"Mud," Charity repeated. "Mud and bees and other assorted bugs. And, I sneeze, which makes my nose red and my eyes water."

"True," Purity agreed. "And, that is so unattractive. You had better marry in the summer or fall." Charity sighed loudly.

"I'll never marry at this rate," she whined, glancing at her mother. "Keven has asked again, you know." Mouse kept her eyes on her dish to keep from laughing. He had turned his affections quickly and pursued Charity over the winter months, much to Mouse's amusement. The depth of his affection for her, or the lack of it, was sufficiently proven to the youngest daughter in the tailor's household.

"No word is better than a refusal," Constance pointed out. "I did not expect to hear from Ravenwood until after the thaw. Is there no strawberry jam, girl?" She glared at Mouse.

"It was finished off yesterday morning," Mouse answered quietly. "This is what we have left." Constance snorted as she spread the apple butter thickly on her third piece of bread.

"You… I mean, I didn't put up enough last summer," she observed, glancing at her husband to see if he noticed her slip. "A miscalculation that will be corrected this year." She took a big bite of her bread and chewed noisily. "You may accept Keven," she continued, her mouth still full as she glanced at Charity. "Just tell him that the wedding will have to wait a bit, until Ravenwood accepts Purity." Charity pouted at her mother.

"And, if he doesn't accept her?" she demanded. "Then, what? Keven will not wait forever." Knowing Keven as he did, Mouse doubted he was waiting for anything but kept her thoughts to herself as she began to clear the table. As the others filed from the room, John took his daughter's hand as she reached his side of the table.

"You have grown even more beautiful over the winter months, little mouse," he said, kissing her hand. The gesture reminded her of Shadow and she blushed. Thinking it was from his compliment, John smiled at her. "You will attract even more attention this year than last. When the others are settled, is there a man you would choose in the village?" Mouse cast her eyes downward to avoid her father's hopeful smile.

"No," she answered truthfully. "There is no one for me in the village. And, Constance…" Mouse bit her lip and glanced up to see her father's eyebrows raised at her.

"And, Constance thinks to keep you here doing her work?" he asked, clearly already knowing the answer. "Aye, Mouse, I know now what has been going on. Can you forgive me for not seeing it sooner? And, perhaps, you will tell me why you did not tell me yourself?" Mouse sighed loudly and sat beside her father.

"She did not wish you to know," she admitted, unwilling to say more. Her father coughed loudly, a condition that had worsened over the cold, raw winter months, and Mouse's eyes filled with concern. He smiled at her as he wiped his mouth with a handkerchief.

"You will continue to help around the house," he instructed her, "but help only." I do prefer your cooking to hers. But, you must not do it all any longer, Mouse. It was wrong of Constance to demand such labor of you and wrong of me not to notice your problem. And, now, don one of your new dresses and let me see just how beautiful you've become. 'Tis the truth, you are the image of your mother at your age." To please her father, Mouse dashed up to the attic and pulled a dress from her wardrobe. Though slightly wrinkled, it was still prettier than Purity's old castoff. The pale blue material complimented her eyes, she thought, as she smoothed her hands over the soft skirt. Pulling the ragged house cap from her head, Mouse dashed back down the stairs.

"Lovely," John said, looking her over. "Do you not feel better dressed this way?" Mouse shrugged, even as she enjoyed her father's pleasure.

"I feel the same way," she confessed. "A dress does not change who I am, Papa." He laughed and then coughed again.

"No, it does not," he agreed. "You are still the most wonderful daughter a man could have. Enjoy the day, Mouse. I will see you at suppertime." He left the house and Mouse turned to find Constance glaring at her. She looked the girl over in her dress and shook her head.

"A silk purse out of a sow's ear," she muttered. "You'll still go to fetch the food and do all the cooking. You'll help the others with the washing and cleaning as well. We'll just see who runs this house." Now, off to the market with you!" Mouse dashed back up to the attic. She pulled the cloak from under her mattress and hid it under her own as she left the house. She was going to visit Ravenwood if she slipped on the ice the entire way.

Chapter Eleven

Mouse stood in the trees, suddenly reluctant to approach the fence. Months had passed since Shadow had come to her room. Though he had kissed her, she now wondered if she had misread his intentions. Perhaps he only sought to comfort her that night. It had been all too easy, all those months apart, to imagine that he meant everything that kiss had seemed to promise. That alone would have kept her warm at night, even without his cloak, and had kept her quiet when Constance baited her. Now, though, she felt foolish for her idle imaginings. Taking a deep breath, she stepped from the forest, deciding that, whatever his intentions, Shadow was still her best friend.

"Ah, you have come at last, Mouse!" Shadow slipped from the trees to greet her almost immediately. "It has been far too long since I saw you last." Mouse smiled shyly.

"It has," she agreed, biting her lip. "Are you well? Is your master well?" Shadow nodded.

"We are all well at Ravenwood," he assured her. "And you, my little mouse, are you well? Was it a difficult winter for you?" Mouse smiled and pulled his cloak from beneath hers.

"Thanks to you, it was quite cozy." She blushed at her other thoughts, even as she held the cloak through the fence. Shadow shook his head.

"It is yours now, Mouse. I gave it to you as a gift." Mouse pulled it back and clutched it to her.

"I slept well beneath it," she said in a small voice, her cheeks flaming.

"That was my intention" he said. "And, did you perhaps think of me when you did so?" Mouse nodded slowly.

"I did. And, Constance did not beat me too many times over the past few months. Papa discovered her deception and now her daughters share some of the work. I am to dress as they do all the time, according to Papa anyway." Shadow took a step closer.

"Does that not please you?"

"I told him it makes no difference what I wear," Mouse said with a shrug. "I am the same person in one dress or the next." Shadow chuckled and Mouse smiled at the familiar sound.

"You are," he agreed. "But may I see this lovely frock he has made for you, even so?" Mouse pulled offer her cloak and turned around for him.

"Do you approve?" she asked with a smirk, feeling like a silly girl for asking. He nodded slowly.

"You are quite beautiful, little mouse," he said, his voice suddenly sounding different. "Is it possible you are even more beautiful than you were when we first met?" Mouse blushed and frowned at him.

"No," she said uncomfortably. "My stepsisters are beautiful. The only person who thinks I am is my father and he has to." Shadow chuckled again.

"Is it permitted for me to think so?" She shrugged and wished to change the subject… quickly.

"Tell me, Shadow," she began, pulling her cloak back on, "did you return safely to Ravenwood that night?" Then, thinking of that night, she blushed again.

"I did," he assured her. "As you see before you. Did you worry terribly about that? I should have found a way to send word to you." Mouse shrugged again.

"I tried to think you were safe, assuming I would hear otherwise if something unpleasant had happened," she said truthfully. "I have missed you terribly, though."

"As I have you, my mouse," Shadow assured her, stepping closer to the fence. "Did something change between us that night, do you think? You seem so uncomfortable with me now. Have I ruined our friendship?

"No!" Mouse answered quickly. "I told you how I felt about you, even before you…" She hesitated and began to wring her hands. "You do know how I feel about you?" Shadow nodded slowly.

"I wonder if you should," he said, barely above a whisper. "You know nothing about me, Mouse. I could be a horrid monster or some evil demon trying to lure an innocent to her doom. You don't know me at all." She laughed at his suggestion.

"I know enough," she said, meaning it. "You are loyal and kind. You are considerate and trustworthy. You care for others before yourself and even risk yourself to protect those you…"

"Love?" he asked. "And, do you know how I feel about you, Mouse? How much I have missed you? How desperately I wanted to come to you again, to see if you were well? Are you so sure of me and what I am? Do you not wonder why you have never seen me? What I might be hiding from you?" Mouse frowned and tried to consider all he was asking.

"I know you care for me," she began thoughtfully. "I know that if you missed me half as much as I have missed you, then you have been most unhappy. I know how many nights I wished to find you in my corner again. I am quite sure of what I know of you. As to the rest, I trust there are good reasons I have never seen you. What could you possibly have to hide from a friend?"

"What indeed, Mouse?" he asked. "Tell me, have you ever wondered what I look like beneath this cloak?" Mouse frowned again.

"I must confess I always think of you just this way," she explained. Then, she laughed at herself. "And I always thought I had a vivid imagination. I know you're very tall and your hands are large and warm, like a man's hands should be. Does it disappoint you that I've not imagined more than that?" Shadow laughed, which helped Mouse relax just a little.

"No, 'tis the truth, it pleases me," he admitted. "If you ever see me, perhaps you will not be too disappointed. Ah, Mouse, I have truly missed you. The day is again beautiful now that I see you." Mouse's smile was wide and bright as she looked at him.

"Do you know, I've tried to think of a good question to ask your master? I've had months to consider what to ask and I have come up completely blank. Isn't that silly? Whenever I tried to think of a good question, all I could think of was..." Mouse blushed suddenly and smile. "All I could think of was you." Shadow stepped closer.

"I must confess that pleases me immensely, my mouse." Mouse could have sworn he was smiling from the sound of his voice. "Perhaps I should assist you in thinking of a question, since I am the cause of your lack of one." Mouse laughed and nodded.

"Well, I would ask to meet him," she teased him, "but that seemed terribly presumptuous. Then I thought to ask what interests him but that seemed too vague." Shadow nodded.

"I see your dilemma," he said thoughtfully. "Mouse stared at him while she tried to think of another question.

"I could ask if he will marry Purity," she said with a wicked look in her eyes. "But that would be rather rude, wouldn't it?" Shadow nodded.

"It would indeed," he agreed. "Though I know he has come to no such decision on any of the offers he has received."

"Is he really all alone, Shadow?" Mouse asked suddenly. "He has you, after all. And, you said *all* were well at Ravenwood. Does that mean he has others like you to serve him?" Shadow was silent for a moment and then folded his hands in front of him.

"There are several who serve the Master of Ravenwood," he said at last. "But, that is not the same thing as having someone with whom to share his life." Mouse considered his answer, being the most he had ever told her.

"So, he is alone and possibly considering marriage," Mouse said, mostly to herself. "Are you?" Shadow started and then put his hands behind his back.

"Am I what, Mouse?"

"Are you all alone?" She heard him let out a sigh.

"I am," he assured her. "I would not have... Mouse, I would never have kissed you if I were not free to do so." She nodded and looked at the ground.

"I didn't really think you would," she said quietly. "It just occurred to me that I might have misunderstood your intent." Shadow stepped closer and was now only a few feet from the fence that loomed between them.

"I kissed you because I care deeply for you, my mouse," he said, his voice deeper suddenly. "Like you, I may not take vows with someone until other matters are settled." Mouse frowned at him.

"Am I permitted to ask how old you are?" she wondered out loud. "You seem so wise and sound so worldly compared to me." Shadow laughed again, and Mouse thought she would never tire of that sound.

"You are wise and mature beyond your years," he said, still chuckling. "And, I am a bit older than your sixteen years. Though, not quite decrepit, I think." Mouse smiled at him.

"I will not be sixteen much longer," she said cheerfully. "And, we have still not thought of a question." Shadow nodded in agreement.

"We should seek to do that," he agreed. "Before you disappear down the path again. You mentioned wanting to know what interests him. What did you mean by that?"

"I wonder what he does for pleasure," Mouse explained. "Just for the simple pleasure of doing something? An interest like that." Shadow nodded.

"I shall ask him that for you," he promised, walking to stand nearer to the fence. "Give me your hand, Mouse." She reached out and put her hand through the fence. Shadow took it and kissed it. He then turned her hand over and kissed her palm, leaving his lips against her skin for a moment. When he released her hand, he turned to go.

"Goodbye for today, my mouse," he said, turning back toward her. "Be well." He disappeared and Mouse looked at her hand before placing it on her cheek. She turned to leave, a bright smile on her face once more.

Chapter Twelve

When her father did not come down to breakfast a few days later, Mouse raced up the stairs to his room. He'd been quiet and sullen for days, his cough worsening, and she'd been so worried about him. She grew even more alarmed to find her father still in his bed.

"You've a fever," she said, feeling his flushed face. "Papa, you're so ill! Has Constance sent for the healer?" He coughed for several minutes and then fell back against his bolster, exhausted from the effort.

"She feels it will pass," he said with a struggle, still breathing hard. Mouse could hear the fluid in his chest with each labored breath.

"I will find her for you," she assured her father. Mouse ran to the village and found the healer, asking her to come at once to the house. After fetching all she needed from the various merchants, she ran through the forest to the fence at Ravenwood.

"Mouse, whatever is wrong?" Shadow asked, even as he appeared.

"My father…." She gasped, still breathing hard from her long run and from her fear. "I cannot stay but wanted you to know why I may not come for a few days." He came to the fence and reached for her hand. When Mouse offered it, he took it and held it to his chest.

"Is there anything you need, my mouse?" She tried to take a deep breath, to still her racing heart.

"I have asked the healer to come," she said, feeling better just for being near her friend. "I don't know what else to do."

"If you need anything, send word to my master," he offered. "He will see you have whatever you need. Promise me, Mouse, you will ask him if you need help." She nodded and he kissed her hand, releasing it. She turned to go and then looked back to see Shadow still watching her.

"Is all well here?" she asked.

"Yes, Mouse, all is well here," he assured her. "Do not forget to take care of yourself, even as you care for your father. You will do him no good if you fall ill yourself. I will wait to hear from you." Mouse dashed back through the forest and ran home.

Chapter Thirteen

Holding a cup to her father's lips, Mouse coaxed him to drink the liquid. She had returned home to find Constance sending the healer away, as if the woman were not truly needed. Mouse had insisted on leading the woman to her father's room, where they found the fever had worsened and John had grown much weaker. He sipped the liquid to please his daughter and then began coughing again.

"She said this will help bring up the fluid," Mouse assured him, putting the cup aside and wiping his chin for him. "You must let it come up to clear your chest." John nodded obediently and then sighed as she put a cool, wet cloth on his burning forehead.

"You've a good way about you, daughter," he whispered, when the next wave of coughing subsided. Mouse smiled as she wiped his mouth.

"We should change your nightshirt," she suggested. "A dry one would be more comfortable and keep you from getting chills." She went to fetch another shirt and took the gray cloak from beneath her mattress. After helping her father change, and struggling not to cry at the sight of his frail body, she tucked the cloak around him like a blanket. Fussing and keeping busy helped her keep her tears at bay. John touched the soft wool and frowned at his daughter.

"Where did you get this?" he asked in confusion. "I have never seen it before." Mouse smiled at him and tucked his arm beneath the cloak.

"When you are completely well, I shall answer that," she said with a wink. "So, you must fight this and get well to satisfy your curiosity." John tried to laugh but coughed instead. Later, when Mouse finished fixing the evening meal, she brought a bowl of rich broth up to her father.

"You must finish this entire bowl," she instructed, spooning the warm broth into his mouth. "To keep your strength up." John pushed her hand away after only a few spoonfuls.

"Let me rest now, Mouse," he said weakly. "Constance will sleep with Purity tonight so that I am not disturbed. Mouse knew it was so Constance was not disturbed that she was sleeping in the other room, but she simply nodded at her father's words. "And, you should find your own bed, Mouse." She put the bowl aside, wiping his chin.

"I will," she assured him, fussing with his covers and the cloak. "You rest now." As John closed his eyes, Mouse added some wood to the fire and sat beside his bed. She picked up her mending basket and sewed long into the night, keeping close watch over her father. Every stitch was a prayer, like a rosary bead, that her father would wake to see the dawn.

Chapter Fourteen

Hearing her father's cough, Mouse rubbed her eyes and moved to sit by him on the bed. His face was far too pale, she thought, and his lips had taken on a bluish tinge, as she felt skin for fever. Wringing out a cloth, she placed it on his forehead and mixed a fresh cup of the herbs left by the healer. Too weak to do so on his own, John let Mouse lift his head to sip the drink.

"Mouse," he gasped. "You must promise that you'll take care of yourself for me." She shook her head and put her finger over his lips.

"Hush now and rest," she whispered. Reaching for a spoon, she tried to get more of the liquid into him.

"Has Constance been in to see me while I slept?" he asked hoarsely. Mouse nodded, not trusting her voice to cover her lie.

"You must rest now, Papa." She fussed with the cloak, making sure he was warm, and then stoked the fire again. She held his hand and wiped his chin when he coughed but she knew he would not last the day.

Chapter Fifteen

Sitting at the table in the dining room, Mouse listened to Constance discuss her plans with her daughters. Her fears had been realized and her father had not lived through that last day. Mouse felt numb and cold and lost without him in their house. She wanted to go to Shadow but had not a single moment to herself to do so.

"…and so we'll send word to Ravenwood immediately," Constance was saying. "We'll let the master know of our situation. Surely he will notify us immediately of his willingness now to marry Purity. And, I'll speak to Keven's father about accepting his suit. He will, of course, take you without a dowry now. As for you," she glanced at Mouse, "you'll settle for whoever will take you." Mouse nodded absently and left the room. She walked up the stairs to the attic and stared out the window toward Ravenwood.

"Charity! Purity! Come here immediately! Girls!" Constance was shouting up the stairs and Mouse heard the others run down to her. She moved down the steps quietly and sat just out of sight, wondering what had happened.

"Girls, this is a messenger from Ravenwood," Constance said, in her most elegant tone. "Sir, will you not remove your cloak?"

"No," came the reply. Mouse held her breath as she recognized Shadow's voice. "I have come to inquire after the health of John the Tailor." Constance feigned tears and wiped her eyes.

"I'm afraid my dear husband has passed on," she said, sniffling into a handkerchief for good measure. "He has left us too soon and with no money to speak of. No dowry for my poor fatherless girls…" She blew her nose. "I was just about to send word to your master regarding my husband's unanswered messages. I thought, perhaps, your master would find it in his heart to accept my Purity now, under such unhappy circumstances."

"My master will meet with her," Shadow told Constance. "Send her to Ravenwood tomorrow at midday. He would speak with her before making his decision. Tell me, madam, are your other daughters well?"

"You see my other daughter before you," Constance replied impatiently. "She is also well and quite beautiful, as you see."

"And, your *other* daughter?" he ask again, equally impatient. Constance sniffed haughtily.

"I have but two daughters," she stated firmly. "And those you see before you, sir. Expect Purity at your gate at midday." Shadow left the house and Mouse ran to the attic to grab her cloak. As she dashed to the kitchen door, she found Constance waiting for her.

"You'll not go anywhere today," she said with a swift blow to the side of Mouse's head. "You will clean out your father's things and scrub the bed to clean it, and air out the room with all the windows open. You will boil anything that touched him and you will remake the bed with clean, fresh linens. Then, you will begin the evening meal. Tonight, you will draw a bath with fresh herbs for each of my daughters. Tomorrow, we go to Ravenwood."

"I thought he only asked to see Purity," Mouse said without thinking, and ducked as Constance swung at her again.

"Impudent chit," she muttered. "You think I would let her go alone to such a place?" She landed another blow to Mouse's head, sending her to the floor on her knees.

Chapter Sixteen

Watching from the shadows as Constance led her daughters to the gate, Mouse saw a cloaked figure open the gate and lead them inside. Racing around the fence to their usual meeting spot, Mouse waited with bated breath. But, Shadow did not come. She hoped he was only detained by the meeting that was taking place and not angry with her for some reason. Having just lost her father, she could not bear the thought of losing her dear friend as well.

She walked slowly back to the house and waited for her stepmother and sisters to return home…

Chapter Seventeen

Mouse set the table and put the food she had prepared out for the evening meal. She filled the cups with milk and went back to the kitchen for some bread. When she returned, she found Constance leading her two daughters into the room.

"Well," Constance said, grabbing the bread from Mouse, "that was the strangest afternoon I have ever spent." Mouse sat down and hoped they would discuss it so she could hear what happened.

"Whatever do you think he wanted?" Purity asked, filling her plate. "I didn't understand half the questions he asked." Constance snorted as she filled her own plate.

"I have no idea," she admitted. "I think he was trying to see how clever you are. And, if you have been raised properly. I'm sure he looked his fill as well and certainly did not find you lacking in that way. I still do not understand why we were not allowed to see him." Mouse kept her eyes averted to hide her surprise. So, they had not seen the Master of Ravenwood after all?

"What difference does it make if I like nice dresses?" Purity asked. "Or, what I do around the house?" Mouse listened closely, picking at her food. "What did he mean by asking about my interests?"

"Clearly he wants to know if you want to marry him only for his gold," Charity said with authority. "And, if you know how to run his household. You lied nicely, I thought." Purity nodded in agreement.

"I did," she agreed with a haughty smile so like her mother's. "What do you think he wanted me to ask him, though? He didn't seem pleased that I asked about the treasure." Constance snorted again.

"You certainly asked enough questions about the estate and his holdings," she said, looking over her daughter to see what possible flaw the master might have seen. "I wonder what else he wanted you to ask?" The discussion continued and Mouse felt as confused as they did by the end of the meal.

Chapter Eighteen

Mouse paced by the fence, hoping Shadow would come. She had been trapped by Constance for days, including one spent in bed from a severe beating. She still sported those bruises and pulled her hood closer to hide them.

"Ah, my mouse, you have come at last." Shadow said, coming all the way to the fence and reaching for her hand. She turned and put her hand in his immediately.

"Shadow… my father…" She began to cry and leaned her head against the fence as he friend kissed her hand.

"I know, little mouse," he said. "I came to your house and learned your news. Why did you not send to my master for help?" She sniffled and wiped her eyes with her free hand.

"I stayed by his side," she explained, trying to find the right words. "There was really nothing to be done, though I tried even so. I tried to…" She began to sob, suddenly feeling safe to cry in earnest, and he put his arms around her through the fence.

"I was not scolding you," he assured her. "I felt so helpless when I learned what had happened. So useless. I asked after you but your stepmother even denied your presence there." Mouse released him and nodded, still wiping her eyes.

"I heard her," she said quietly, her tears still in her voice. "She has kept me too busy to come to you and, when I did come, you were not here."

"I'm sorry," he said, quite sincerely. "There were visitors. You know of their visit?" Mouse nodded again.

"I knew they were coming here. I followed them and came here to our spot. I hoped you stayed away because of their visit and not because you were angry with me." Shadow reached for her hand again.

"How could I be angry with you, my dearest Mouse?" You bring only joy and happiness with you." She sniffled again and looked up at him.

"Are you well, Shadow? And your master? And the others here?" He nodded slowly.

We are all well," he assured her. "But my master was saddened to learn of your father's passing. He again wishes to know if he can do anything for you." Mouse sighed, trying to keep her tears in check.

"I need nothing," she said, smiling a little. "Did you ever ask him my last question? I had forgotten all about it until just now." Shadow nodded.

"I did," he said. "Let me think... he was quite intrigued, as I recall. He thought about it a great deal before answering. He said he finds pleasure in a beautiful sunrise and sunset, and enjoys just sitting quietly watching them. He enjoys a good book, if truly well written, and a good piece of music, when it is inspiring enough to make his heart race. He also enjoys archery, when he has the occasion to practice it, as well as riding a fine horse. But, most especially, he finds pleasure in your questions." Mouse's moist eyes widened, as did her smile.

"All that," she whispered. "He said all that?" 'Tis truly remarkable that he should have thought so much about my question, isn't it? As if it really mattered to him? Your master seems a kind and thoughtful man, Shadow. A man of deep feeling and sensitivity. I think he may be much like you." Shadow chuckled.

"You pay me quite a compliment, my mouse," he said, his voice deeper again. "And, if his answer pleases you, his question should as well." Mouse held her breath in anticipation. "He asks what pleases you? In what do you find pleasure, little mouse?" She sighed and looked at the ground very conscious of the fact that he still held her hand.

"I agree with all this thoughts," she said slowly, wanting to give him as good and genuine an answer in return. "Though I've never shot an arrow or ridden a horse. I think babies are wonderful as well as newborn animals. I like genuine smiles and honest laughter. I like a warm kitchen on a cold day and the first apple of the season and the way strawberries taste like summer sunshine. Most especially, though, I like you." She smiled at him suddenly and he tightened his grip on her hand.

"Oh, Mouse," he sighed. "If only…" He bowed his head and kissed her hand, keeping it to his lips for a long time.

"I didn't mean to make you sad," she said quickly, thinking she had said the wrong thing. He lifted his head a little and sighed again.

"You could never make me sad, Mouse. And I shall tell my master your answers. I am sure he will be delighted with them. Tell me, do you have another question? He looks forward to them now with great anticipation."

"Oh, how wonderful and awful that is!" she cried. "Now I must try to make my questions clever enough to please him." Shadow laughed and shook his head.

"No, you must ask only what your heart wants to know. He will see any contrivance you attempt. I am certain he would willingly forgo a question rather than have a false one." Mouse nodded with a frown.

"You are right, of course. It just seems such a responsibility, doesn't it? I had thought to ask him about his meeting with Purity but now feel I should not."

"What were you going to ask about the meeting, Mouse?" She looked at him and bit her lip, feeling suddenly she should not have mentioned it.

"They didn't understand his questions," she explained. "I'm not really sure of everything he asked but they didn't understand what he was trying to learn from them. And, he seemed to be waiting for Purity to ask him something specific. Would he explain it to you, for me?"

"No, Mouse, he will not. The master sought to learn of Purity's heart from his questions and her answers. The question he sought was one she could not offer. It is not my place to explain it to you." She nodded and he squeezed her hand. "Will you forgive me for not telling you more?"

"There is nothing to forgive," she told him truthfully. "I only asked because I was wondering if he would decide to marry her after all. He seems so kind and gentle I cannot imagine him with Purity, Shadow. I know it's awful of me to say so but it is the truth of it, just the same. She could never love him better than herself."

"And that is important, Mouse?"

"I would think so," she replied with another frown. "How else can you give yourself to someone? If you only think of yourself, there is no room for another in a marriage." Shadow chuckled and kissed her hand again.

"More sage wisdom from my beautiful mouse," he said, and she could hear his amusement in his voice.

"What gives *you* pleasure, Shadow?" She felt him hold her hand to his warm cheek.

"Many of the same things you and my master like. You, precious mouse, most especially have brought pleasure and beauty into my life." She wanted to run her fingers over his face but feared he would pull away. "What are you thinking, Mouse, when you stare at me so intently?" She started and smiled shyly.

"That I wanted to touch your face," she said honestly. "Since I can't see it, I thought… but I did not want to betray your trust." He turned her palm to his cheek and held it there.

"One day, perhaps you will do more than that. But, for now, we must take only what we can." He kissed her palm, still holding it against his face. "Can you think of another question to ask today?" Overwhelmed by his touch, Mouse swallowed hard and tried to think of anything.

"I'm trying to think of one," she said wistfully, "but, I find it difficult to think with you…" He chuckled again and pulled her hand from his face.

"That was selfish of me. Is this better?" He still held her hand in his. She nodded slowly.

"For thinking," she agreed, "if not for being near you." He chuckled again and squeezed her hand. "I cannot think today, Shadow. Could you explain to him for me? Tell him I asked if he is well and that I felt so overwhelmed being near you again that I couldn't think of a question. Will he be disappointed in me, do you think?" Shadow shook his head.

"I think he will understand. You have only just lost your father, Mouse. He would not expect anything but that you think of your loss. He knows of our feelings for one another and will understand that as well. Will you not remove your hood, so I may see you today? It has been too many days since I've looked at you. Mouse shook her head and took a step back.

"No, not today. Do not ask me today." Shadow tightened his grip on her hand when she tried to pull it away.

"What has frightened you, Mouse? Or, are you angry with me for asking this of you when I cannot offer the same gift?" She shook her head and her hood fell back. She heard his in-drawn breath, even as she turned away. "Who has hurt you so?" He gently pulled on her hand to draw her nearer. She closed her eyes and his warm fingers traced lightly over her bruised skin.

"It was my fault. I was slow to clear the table one night and sassed her the next morning. I should have held my tongue." Mouse thought she heard him growl.

"Mouse, you could never deserve to be hurt, no matter what you say. She has no leave to treat you so. No one has the right to hurt another in such a way. The master will…" Mouse's eyes widened fearfully.

"Please don't tell him," she begged. "Please, Shadow, promise you won't tell him."

"How can you ask this of me?" He traced on very purple bruise. "He demands and deserves my complete honesty and respect. He cares for you and would be appalled by this treatment of you. He would be equally appalled should I keep it from him, Mouse. Something must be done to protect you and he is the one to see it done. Would you deny him that?" Mouse's eyes filled with tears.

"But he has so much else to consider," she said, hardly above a whisper. "So many things that are much more important than I am to think about. And, you have so much to keep you occupied in serving him. Surely, this can be disregarded. I will hold my tongue and keep things in order and it shall never happen again, Shadow. Tell him that, will you, for me?" He pulled her closer and lifted her chin with his fingers.

"Close your eyes, my precious mouse," he whispered. She obeyed and he kissed again, a long, slow, soft kiss that left Mouse breathless. Then, he kissed each bruise on her face. When he released her, he kissed her forehead again. "I will tell him for you, Mouse." When she opened her eyes, he had stepped back.

"Shadow, if you ever need anything, you have only to ask me," she said, pulling her hood back up over her head.

"I need only you, my beloved mouse. Be well until I see you again."

Chapter Nineteen

Constance stood staring at the cloaked figure in the doorway. He refused to enter the house or to remove his hood. She glared at him as he spoke.

"...and, therefore, the Master of Ravenwood respectfully suggests that Miss Purity seek marriage with a man in the village. If you wish, he would be willing to speak with your other daughters, perhaps finding a suitable match with one of them." Constance crossed her arms and considered how to answer. She certainly couldn't say what she was thinking, even she knew that.

"I have but one other daughter," she said finally, wondering at the messenger's constant insistence otherwise. "Charity is promised to another but would be willing to meet your master to talk with him. He must show himself this time, however. No more shadows and tricks of the light. She should know what she is getting in the same bargain, should she not?"

"The Master does as he sees fit, madam. If you feel this way, perhaps it is best that the meeting not take place." He turned to leave and Constance let out an exasperated sigh.

"When should she come to him?" The messenger turned back to her.

"Tomorrow at noon," he instructed. "And, the third daughter the following day." He left before she could protest and Constance slammed the door. Climbing the stairs, she gave Charity the news. Then, she climbed to the third floor. Mouse heard her heavy steps and barely had time to hide the cloak and straighten her mattress before Constance threw open the door.

"Why does the Master of Ravenwood insist that I have three daughters?" she demanded, looking around the room as if expecting to find some hidden secret. Her eyes then traveled slowly over Mouse, who sat brushing her long blond hair.

"He knew of Papa," Mouse offered. "Perhaps..." Constance snorted and walked to the window.

"He expects you to go to meet him the day after tomorrow. He meets Charity tomorrow. I will expect you to perform poorly to better her chances." Mouse gaped at her stepmother.

"Why does he wish me to come? Surely Charity will know what to say and he will be impressed with her beauty." Constance turned to face her late husband's child.

"Of course he will be impressed with her," she said with a sniff. "But, you will insure her success by appearing addled and stupid. Know this, Mouse. You will not find yourself the bride of Ravenwood." The woman left the room, slamming the door for good measure, and Mouse threw herself in the bed. She had no desire to be the bride of Ravenwood.

Chapter Twenty

Mouse stood beside her stepmother in a huge marble hall. She wore one of Purity's old dresses under her old cloak and her hands were shaking as she fisted them against her skirt. The tall cloaked figure that met them at the gate did not speak so Mouse had no idea if it was Shadow or not. Behind the iron gate, Mouse had discovered there were beautiful gardens that, on another day, would have taken her breath away. Lush and ancient, the place was alive with color, along with humming bees and fluttering butterflies. Trees were filled with fruit and songbirds. It was a place of beauty and magic, if only Mouse had been able to enjoy it.

They passed through wooden doors she felt must have been built for giants. Glancing around the hall, she saw no portraits to identify the man who ruled Ravenwood. There were beautiful paintings but Mouse was too nervous to inspect them.

Constance had kept Mouse under close watch, leaving Purity to watch over her when Charity had come to this same place for her appointment. They left in much the same turmoil as they had on the previous visit, still wondering what the man wanted from them. Mouse had desperately wanted to talk to Shadow before meeting his master but had been unable to slip away. The hours had passed all too quickly and, now, here she was.

"You will seek to displease him, Mouse," Constance hissed in her ear. "Remember what I said. Nothing will come of this, so seek to please me in this matter or I shall make you rue this day." Mouse looked up at her, already ruing the day.

"I am not a good liar," she reminded her stepmother, "as you have often pointed out. I will do my best to avoid answering the way he wants but he is sure to know if I lie to him."

"Lie then," Constance instructed her. "It will disappoint him and he will send you packing." Another huge door opened in a far wall and Constance shoved Mouse toward it. "Remember what I said and what I can do to you." Mouse walked slowly toward the doorway and peered through.

Constance pushed her and Mouse walked slowly into a room that was even larger than the hall she'd just left. Brilliant sunshine flowed through the largest windows she'd ever seen. She was certain she could see for miles out those windows and would have liked to stare out for house to see the sunset. That made her think of Shadow and she glanced around, spying a darkened wall opposite her. Several steps rose from the floor and a large chair sat on a landing at the top. There was someone seated in the chair and a cloaked figure stood to the left, but she could make out no more than that.

Mouse walked toward the steps at Constance's urging, until the man put up his hand. She could not see his face in the shadows, nor make out much about him, and Mouse now knew why her stepmother had been disappointed in her previous visits. Mouse curtsied awkwardly and stood slowly.

"Why do you bow before me, little mouse?" a deep voice asked. It seemed muffled somehow and Mouse wondered if he were trying to disguise his voice as he hid in the shadows.

"Does one not bow to one's betters?" she asked. Constance poked her in the back. The man laughed a little.

"Am I your better, Mouse?" She considered her answer.

"In this instance, it seemed wise to assume so and to show you my respect." She could hear Constance's annoyed breathing behind her.

"Remove your cloak, little one." Mouse did and Constance took it from her. "Why do you come to me dressed this way? Most would wear their finest dresses to impress me." Mouse took a deep breath.

"A dress is just a dress," she said slowly. "It does not change one's heart." Constance snorted behind her and poked her again for good measure.

"Tell me, do you like my house?" he asked. "Would it please you to live here?" Mouse looked around the room and then back at him.

"Not if I had to wash the windows," she answered truthfully. She heard the man laugh again and fought a smile of her own. "But I would like to watch the sunset from those wonderful windows."

"Ah, yes, the sunset. An interest we share, I think. It is, in fact, a lovely view from here. Perhaps I shall watch it with you someday. Tell me, Mouse, are you happy?" She looked at her hands for a moment and then took another deep breath.

"Most of the time, I am," she told him. "My father is gone now and that makes it more difficult. But, he always told me it is a good day if you wake up, so I try to remember that each morning. And, there is so much to enjoy, I try to be happy for his sake." Constance grunted behind her. Mouse wasn't sure that was good or bad.

"And, if you could have anything you wanted, what would you ask for, Mouse?"

"Nothing," she said quickly, forgetting that Constance wanted her to lie. Ah, well, in for a penny... "You cannot give me back my father, nor can you grant my dearest wish, I think. So, I would ask nothing from you." He was quiet for a moment.

"Do you have anything you would like to ask me, Mouse?" She smiled brightly at that question.

"How are you, on this beautiful day? Are you well and happy, sir?" He laughed loudly at that, and clapped his hands together.

"I am well, Mouse. I am very well and trying to be happy each day, just as you are. I would like to ask you one more thing before you leave me, though. Would you like to be the mistress of Ravenwood? Would you consider becoming my wife?"

Chapter Twenty-One

"And, then, she looked at him and told him in no uncertain terms that she would not!" Constance concluded her story with a firm nod. "The cheeky chit said no to the Master of Ravenwood." Both Charity and Purity stared at their stepsister in horror.

"Are you mad?" Purity asked. "Why ever would you say no to being the wife of such a man?" Mouse just shrugged as she pushed her untouched plate aside.

"You told me to," she said, glancing at Constance. "Didn't he ask each of you if that was what you wanted?" Constance was still glaring at her. She'd been angry since they left the estate and made sure that Mouse knew it.

"He asked earlier in the interview if they were there for the purpose of seeking a husband," Constance said, clearly confused with the entire nonsense. "He did not ask them in the same way he asked you. Do you know, I had the distinct impression that he would have married you if you had agreed?"

"But, Mother, if she did, then she could ask him for large dowries for us," Purity pointed out, already trying to reason out a way to make this all work in her favor. "Since it seems neither of us will have him, shouldn't we make the most of this situation? Force her to say yes and we could ask for a large bride price as well. If he wants her, let him pay for her. She'd finally be worth something..." Constance stared at Mouse in a most unsettling way.

"Clear the table, Mouse," she said, a slow, disturbing smile spreading across her face. "And, scrub the kitchen floor when you've finished the dishes."

Chapter Twenty-Two

Word spread quickly through the village that Mouse had accepted the proposal of the Master of Ravenwood. She only learned the news herself when she went to the village one morning, finally free of Constance's watchful eyes.

"Sold yourself to the highest bidder, then, did you?" Keven sneered, as he looked her over with disgust. "So, you were up to something up there, after all?" Mouse smirked at him.

"I did no such thing," she informed him, trying to get passed him.

"Everyone's talking about it," he continued, undeterred by her denial. "Gifts are being bought, to win your favor and his. Clothes are being cleaned and pressed, in anticipation of being invited to a great wedding. You are all anyone is talking about." Mouse suddenly realized he was serious and she began to panic. "And, your stepmother is rubbing her hands together at the thought of all that gold she has been promised for you. Gold for her and dowries for the others. Now, I find myself competing for Charity's hand, when I held it so easily just yesterday." Mouse's eyes filled with tears when she considered just what her stepmother might have done. She pushed passed Keven and raced through the village and the woods to the fence.

"Shadow!" she called, her voice desperate. "Shadow! Please come to me! Please!" He stepped from the bushes but did not come any closer.

"What is it, Mouse?" She gripped the uprights and stared at him.

"Please, Shadow, tell me what has happened?" He shrugged.

"You know what has happened, Mouse. You have agreed to marry my master if he gives your stepmother gold and large dowries for your stepsisters. You have found a way out of your misery at last. Are you not pleased with this decision?" Mouse gasped and gripped the iron bars tighter to keep from falling down.

"No," she whispered. "I did no such thing. I told your master that I did not wish to marry him. Weren't you there? Didn't you hear me? I told him he could not grant my dearest wish and I told him that I did not wish to marry him."

"I heard you," he said coldly. "And, then we received your message. You had changed your mind, you said. You thought it over and would like to live in his beautiful house and be his wife and watch his sunsets, as long as your family would be taken care of. You were most specific in your demands and he agreed eagerly to meet them. You see, Mouse, all those times he heard about you, from me, all those questions you asked and things you felt, he must have fallen in love with you. Your kind, sweet, innocent heart touched him and he now seems to want you for his own. Has he not made it clear he would meet any demand you make, to make you his?"

"No," she protested weakly. "No, Shadow, I did not do this. You know me. I would not say such things. I do not care for such things. I don't want him or his gold. How can you think I would do this?" Shadow turned to leave and then turned back.

"It was disappointing to learn that I was so wrong about you, Mouse. You even wore my cloak to deliver your message, with no thought to my feelings when you spoke to me of your change of heart. You did not ask if it were I, standing there. It was as if you didn't even know me... or want to. To deny it now seems to confirm your fickle nature, does it not?

"In spite of everything, though, I wish you every happiness, and, when the time comes that you marry my master, I will live to serve you as I serve him. But, from that day forward, we will no longer be Mouse and Shadow. We will only be mistress and servant. Be well, little mouse." He disappeared and Mouse sank to her knees, her face in her hands. Perhaps the ground would swallow her up... or perhaps this was all just a bad dream and she would wake soon, relieved it was not true...

Chapter Twenty-Three

The ground held firm, unfortunately for Mouse, and it was no dream. Every day for two weeks, Mouse went to the gate of Ravenwood and asked to speak with the master. Every single time, she was denied and told she would see him at the wedding. That day came, far too quickly and despite Mouse's prayers to the contrary. Constance saw her up, bathed, and dressed, threatening her every step of the way and forcing her when Mouse would have refused.

"I will hold a knife to your back, if I have to," Constance hissed, as she dragged Mouse through the front door. "And bind and drag you to get you there. You will speak your vows and wed the man today and then all shall be well. Just think, you are free of me as soon as you do."

"But I do not wish to marry him," Mouse told her for the hundredth time. Constance gripped her arm so roughly, Mouse cried out as she was dragged down the street. Everyone in the village followed them, as was the custom, wanting to witness the marriage and hoping to enjoy a lavish celebration. A cloaked figure met them at the gate and only admitted Mouse and her family. He led them silently through the front hall to the great room where the master had interviewed Mouse and her sisters. A man stood in front of the large windows but the sun was so bright Mouse could not make out his face. A priest joined the man and another cloaked figure moved to stand beside the priest. Constance shoved Mouse suddenly and she stumbled. The cloaked man grabbed her arm gently, helping her from the ground.

"Thank you, Shadow." He nodded and released her arm.

"Do you come of your own free will?" the priest asked. Mouse shook her head and Constance moved to her side, squeezing her arm painfully.

"Say the words, Mouse," she hissed, "or live to regret it." Shadow moved quickly to pull Constance away from Mouse.

"You may speak freely," the master instructed her. She peered closely at him, still unable to see his face for the light behind him.

"I do not come freely," she said, her voice small in the large room. "I did not accept you. My stepmother sent that message to you, hoping to gain from this marriage what she could not gain from her own daughters. I truly care for you, sir, as I have come to know you over this past year. But, I cannot marry you, as I do not love you." Mouse bowed her head and sobbed silently, knowing she had let everyone down and somehow disappointed the one person she cared for most.

"Then why come here, Mouse?" the master asked. "If you did not come to marry me, why come at all?" She sniffled and wiped her nose on the sleeve of her fine dress.

"Constance brought me, insisting that I marry you, but I cannot. She accepted your proposal, not I. I'm sorry!" Mouse ran from the room and through the great all to the outside. Seeing everyone still waiting at the gate, she dashed around the side of the huge house, lifting her skirts to run faster. On and on, she ran until she found herself stopped by the fence. Only, this time, she was on the inside looking out.

"You cannot go any further, Mouse." She turned to see Shadow standing behind her.

"Please go away," she whispered. "I can't bear to look at you right now."

"Why not, Mouse? Am I so distasteful now that you have met my master?" Mouse clenched her fists and glared at him.

"How can you even ask me that, after what just happened? Don't you understand? I can't marry him because I love you, Shadow. That was my dearest wish, you see, to be yours at last. How can you think I could find you distasteful? You could be pockmarked, hunchbacked, foul-smelling, one-eyed, toothless, and three feet tall and I would still love you." She turned back to the fence and gripped it tightly, leaning her forehead against the cool metal uprights.

"Then why do you wish me to leave you, little one?" Mouse sighed loudly but didn't turn around.

"Because I disappointed you. It hurts to lose you but it hurts so much more that you don't believe in me any longer. I would understand if you loved someone else but you believe in lies instead of my love. You believe I care more for things and for myself more than I care for you. I can't see your eyes but I know they no longer look at me warmly. I know you no longer smile beneath your hood. I know you no longer wish to touch me the way I want you to. I can't bear your contempt any longer."

"Oh, Mouse. Dear, dear Mouse. You said you didn't imagine what I looked like and, yet you describe my face when I look at you?" She shrugged, the pain in her heart unbearable.

"I could hear it in your voice," she said, closing her eyes against her tears. "I didn't need to see your face to know what you looked like when you looked at me."

"Mouse, please, come to me." She turned and looked at him. "Please, Mouse…" She walked slowly to him and stood right in front of him. He took her hand and placed it on his cheek. "The Master of Ravenwood has much to offer you, Mouse. Would you not be happier with all he has, if I would still be your friend? If we could still be Mouse and Shadow, would you reconsider marrying him?" She shook her head.

"No," she whispered, her tears falling freely now. "I cannot be his wife. If I cannot be with you, I will be with no one." She pulled her hand away but Shadow grabbed it back. He moved her fingers over his cheek, touching his lips, his nose, his eyes, and his forehead. He took her other hand, bringing that up to his face as well. Mouse stepped closer as she touched him and Shadow pushed back his hood. His blond, wavy hair gleamed in the sunshine, as his bright blue eyes sparkled at her. His handsome face smiled as she stared up at him, amazed to see him at last.

"Then, precious Mouse, we must see that you have your dearest wish." He took her hand and led her back to the house, bringing her back to the room to stand by the windows. The priest stood waiting, along with Mouse's family and the man she had just rejected. She glanced at him, hoping he was not terribly angry with her. Instead, she found a warm smile waiting for her and she glanced from him to Shadow and back again, her question in her eyes.

"My father, Mouse," Shadow explained with a sheepish grin. "The Master of Ravenwood." Mouse blinked at him and then turned to the older man.

"And you wished to marry me?" she asked in confusion. He laughed and shook his head.

"No," he assured her, taking her by the shoulders. "I asked only if you wished it. You see, I wished my son to marry for love and he could not find that if every girl only wished to marry the heir of Ravenwood. He needed to find the one girl who would marry him only for himself. The fence you wondered about, the treasure it guarded? It is my son I sought to protect. He is the treasure of Ravenwood. Now, Mouse, will you agree to marry today, if I grant your heart's dearest wish?" Mouse looked back at Shadow, who held out his hand.

"And, can you forgive me for doubting you, Mouse?" She took his hand and smiled up at him.

"Yes and yes!" she agreed. They turned together toward the priest.

"Do you come of your own free will?" he asked Mouse. She beamed, brighter than the sunshine streaming in through the windows.

"I do," she said, smiling up at Shadow. Then, she frowned at him. "But, what should I call you?" He laughed and slipped his arm around her waist, pulling her closer.

"I prefer Shadow and Mouse, at least a little longer." Mouse agreed and followed the priest through the vows. The Master of Ravenwood kept his word, despite Constance's deception, and provided the bride price and dowries as agreed. The people of the village were indeed treated to a lavish and happy celebration.

And, Shadow and Mouse? They watched the sun set through the windows on their first day as husband and wife and then lived happily ever after, of course…

14510502R00056

Made in the USA
San Bernardino, CA
28 August 2014